In the Country

For Rose and Mike

OXFORD
UNIVERSITY PRESS

Great Clarendon Street, Oxford OX2 6DP.
United Kingdom

Oxford University Press is a department of the University of Oxford.
It furthers the University's objective of excellence in research, scholarship,
and education by publishing worldwide. Oxford is a registered trade mark of
Oxford University Press in the UK and in certain other countries

First published 2001
Revised edition 2007
This new edition 2017

British Library Cataloguing in Publication Data

Data available

ISBN: 978-0-19-275903-0

10 9 8 7 6 5 4 3 2 1

Paper used in the production of this book is a natural,
recyclable product made from wood grown in sustainable forests.
The manufacturing process conforms to the environmental
regulations of the country of origin.

Printed in China

For school
Discover eBooks, inspirational
resources, advice and support

For home
Helping your child's learning
with free eBooks, essential
tips and fun activities

www.oxfordowl.co.uk

We're going on a **word** hunt...

In the Country

farmhouse   honey   anemone   boots   gull   wheat

BENEDICT BLATHWAYT

OXFORD
UNIVERSITY PRESS

This is where we live

field

valley

wood

village

stream

waterfall

cliff

forest

beach

hill

road

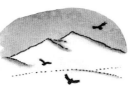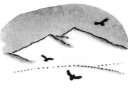

mountain

This is our farm

barn

farmhouse

stable

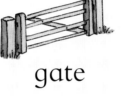

gate

cow shed

pond

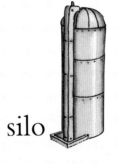

silo

sheep-dip

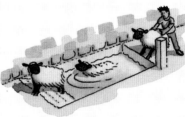

fence

wall

hen house

bridge

7

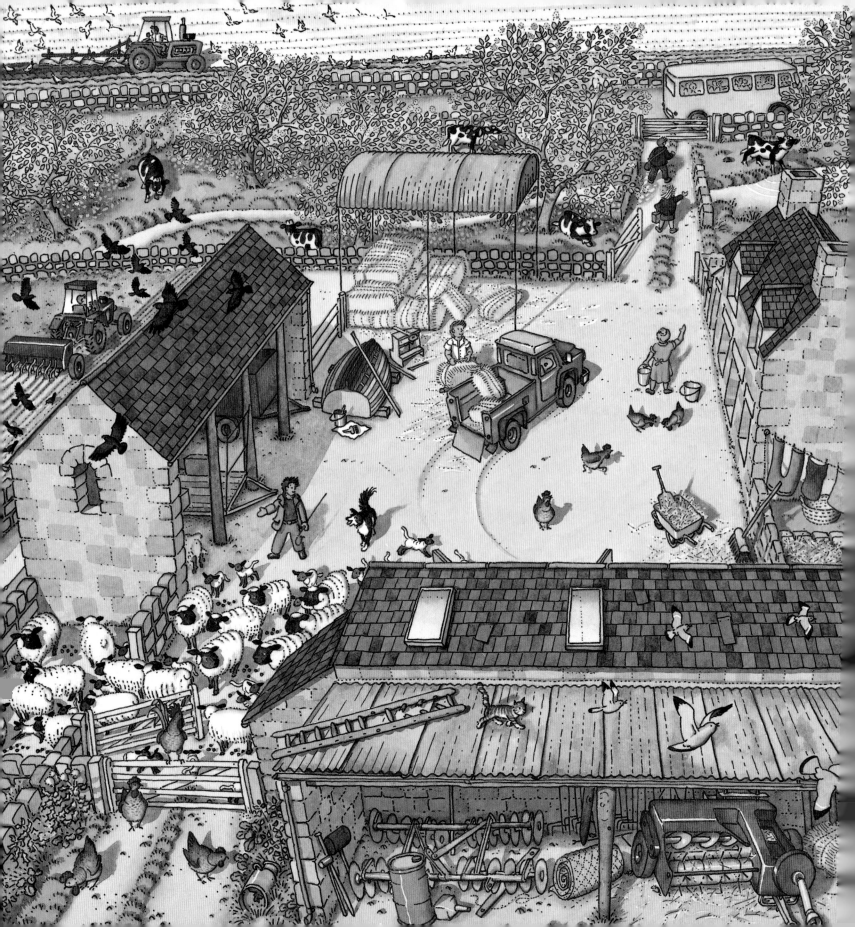

There is work for us all

bucket

sheepdog

plough

seed drill

wheelbarrow

broom

tractor

baler

hoe

shovel

shepherd

pick-up truck

rake

fork

Spring is here

blossom

shoots

frog

lamb

dragonfly

bumblebee

caterpillar

duckling

frog spawn

bud

nest

rainbow

tadpoles

ladybird

11

Animals around the farm

sheep

rabbit

hen

duck

cockerel

cow

pony

swallow

cat

fox

deer

hawk

A trip in the boat

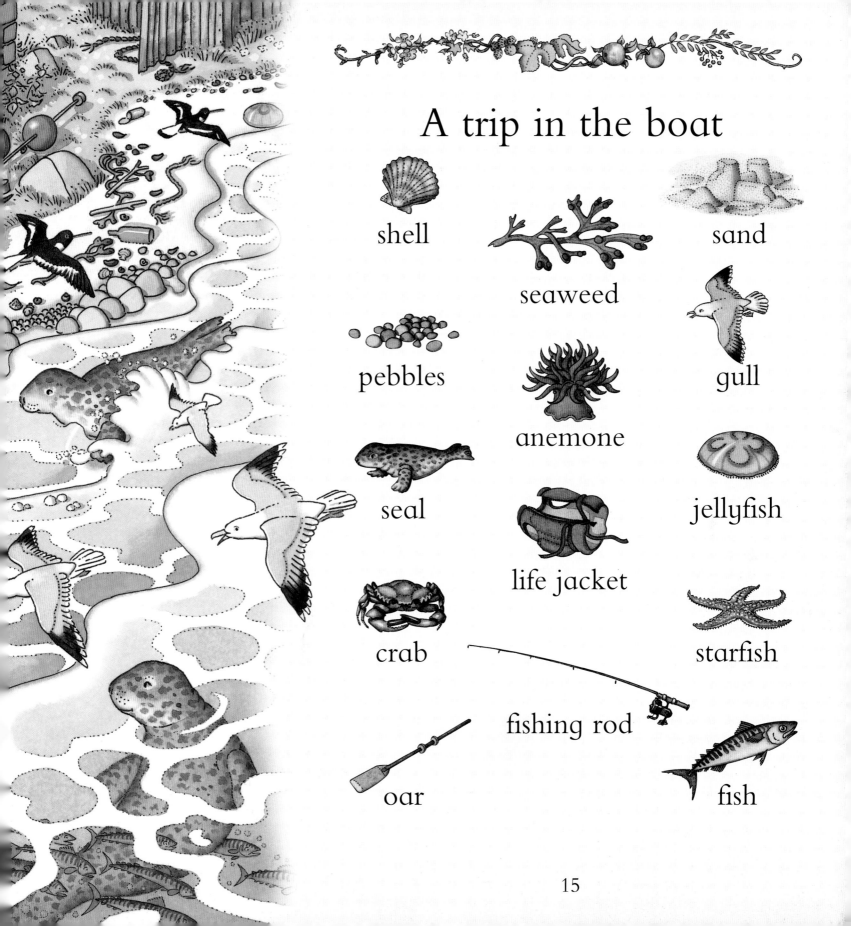

shell

seaweed

sand

pebbles

anemone

gull

seal

life jacket

jellyfish

crab

starfish

fishing rod

oar

fish

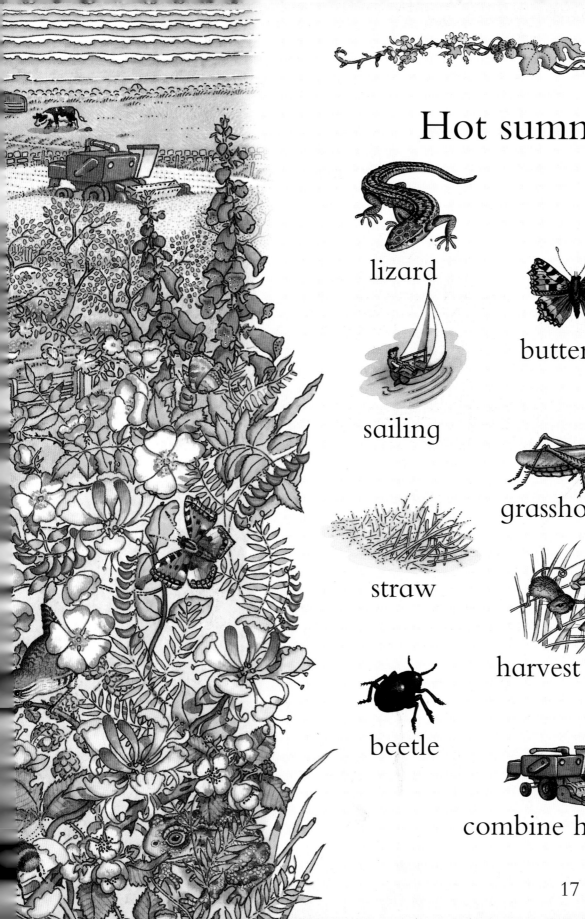

Hot summer days

lizard

swimming

butterfly

sailing

wheat

grasshopper

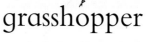
straw

poppy

harvest mice

beetle

pheasant

combine harvester

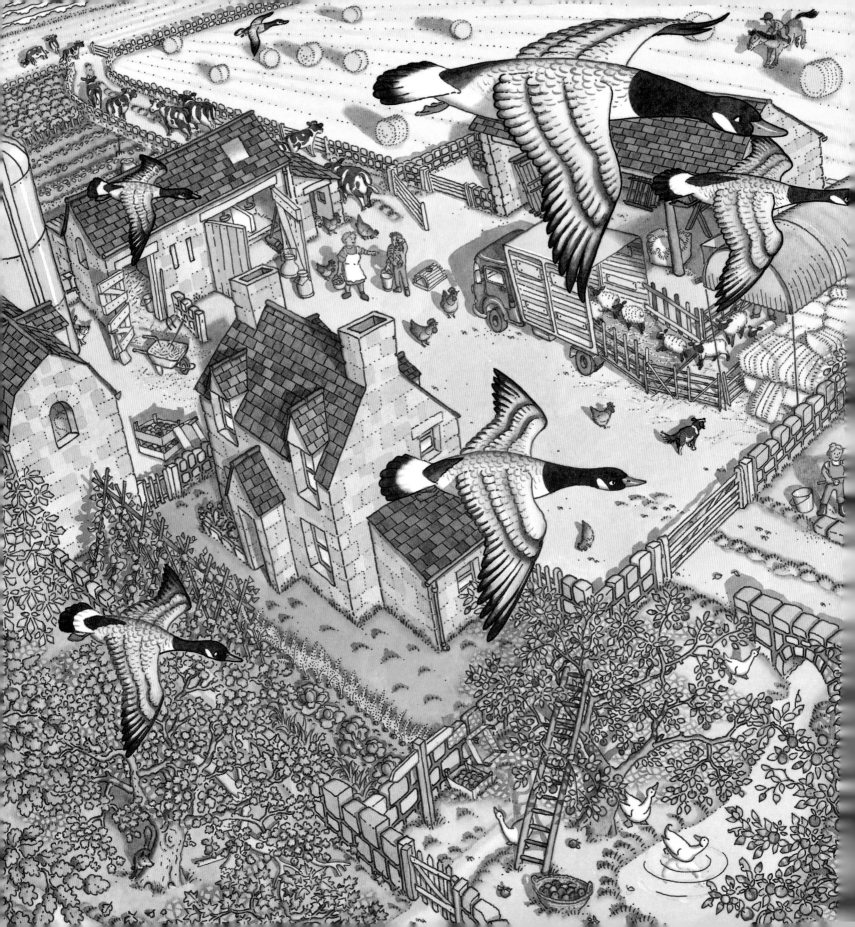

Food from our farm

eggs

potatoes

milk

cheese

honey

pumpkin

apples

maize

cabbage

carrots

beans

apple juice

Autumn evening

bonfire

blackberry

hazelnut

mouse

wood pigeon

squirrel

chestnut

toadstool

rosehip

geese

autumn leaves

acorn

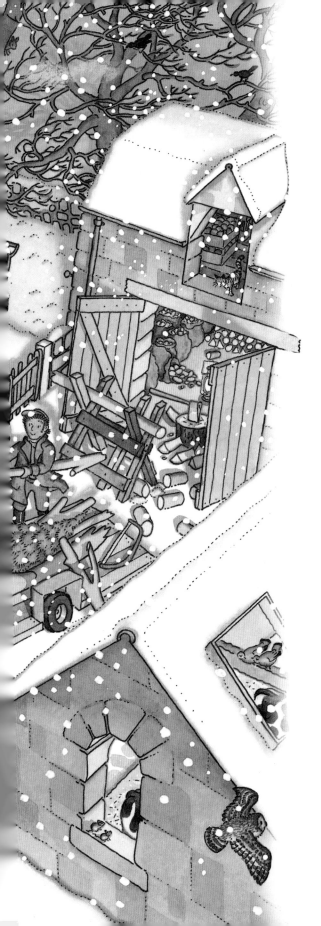

When winter winds blow

snow

ice

lamp

logs

boots

hay bale

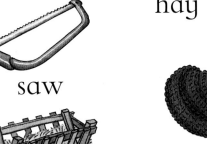

saw

woollen hat

axe

manger

owl

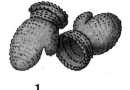

gloves

We're going on a word hunt

Can you match the words to the pictures?

(Answers are on the next page.)

hawk

pebbles

cow

gull

sheepdog

cow shed

fox

seal

stream

farmhouse

combine harvester

sheep

bridge

bonfire

cliff

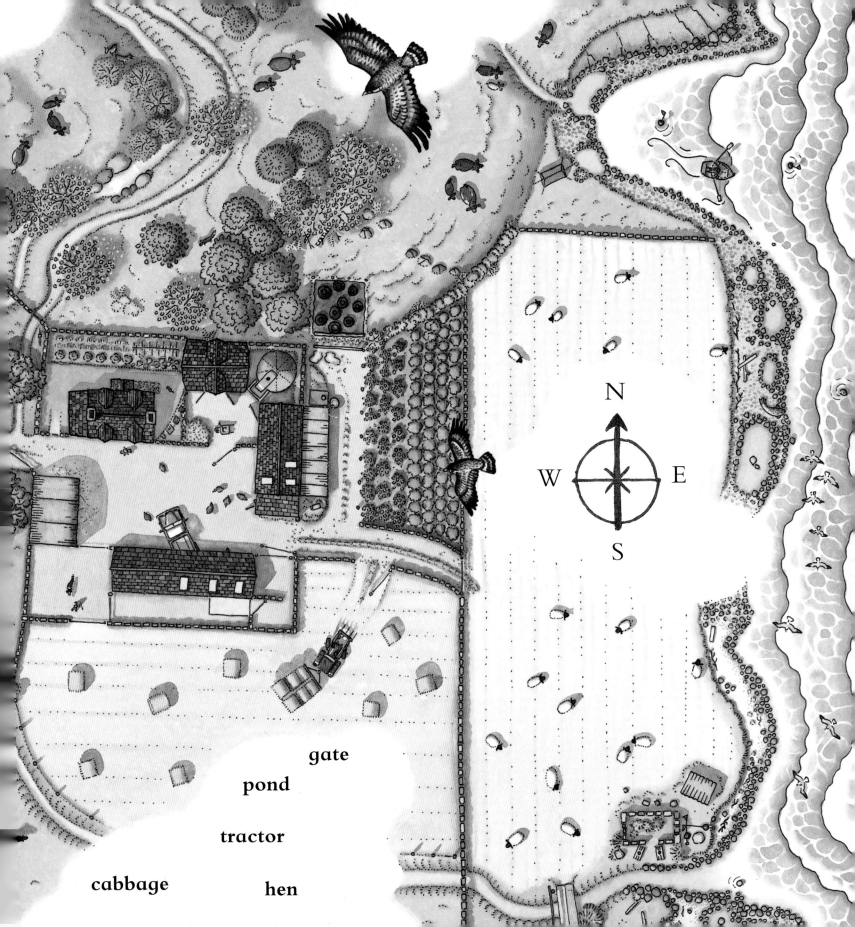

gate

pond

tractor

cabbage hen

We're going on a word hunt
Can you match the words to the pictures?

(Answers)

combine harvester

pond

bridge

bonfire

cow

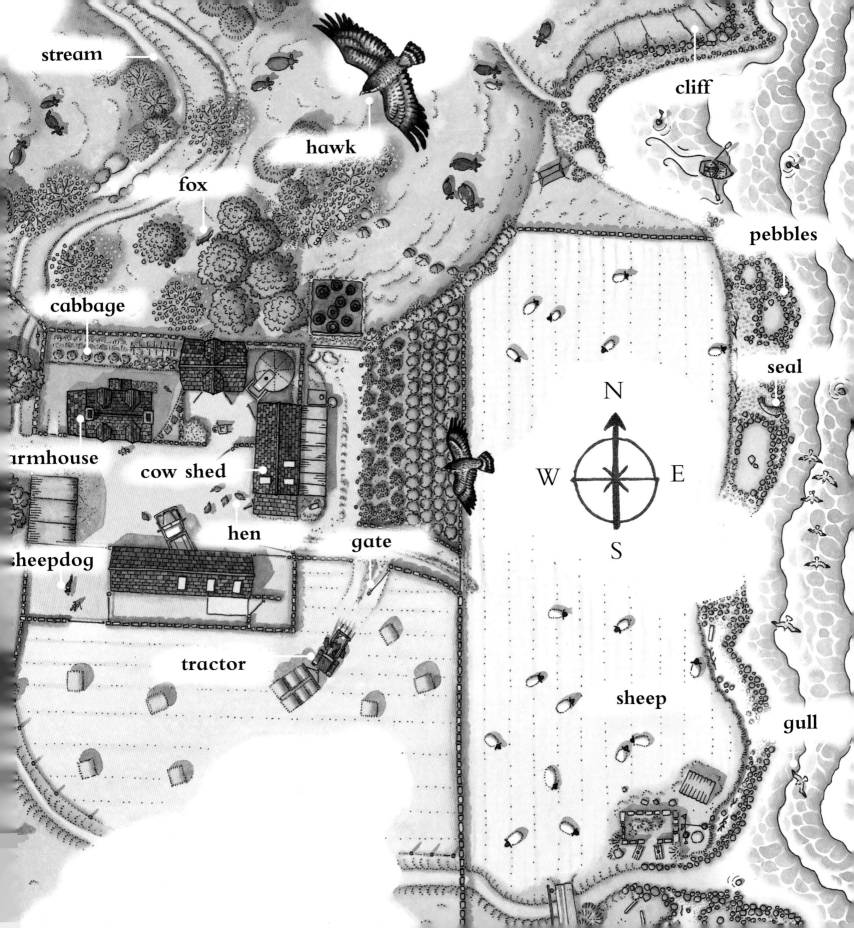

stream

hawk

cliff

fox

pebbles

cabbage

seal

farmhouse

cow shed

hen

gate

N

W E

S

sheepdog

tractor

sheep

gull

We're going on a word hunt
Can you find these words in the book?

(Look in the index to find the right page.)

Going for a walk

boots   rainbow   fence

autumn leaves

field   village

bridge

sand

Animals

rabbit

duckling

ladybird   wood pigeon

jellyfish   lizard   squirrel

owl

Plants

acorn

blossom   poppy

blackberry

wheat

pumpkin   bud

seaweed

On the farm

wheelbarrow   stable

eggs

logs

cockerel

tractor

pony

manger

Index

J

jellyfish 15

L

ladybird 11
lamb 11
lamp 23
life jacket 15
lizard 17
logs 23

M

maize 19
manger 23
milk 19
mountain 5
mouse 21

N

nest 11

O

oar 15
owl 23

P

pebbles 15
pheasant 17

pick-up truck 9
plough 9
pond 7
pony 13
poppy 17
potatoes 19
pumpkin 19

R

rabbit 13
rainbow 11
rake 9
road 5
rosehip 21

S

sailing 17
sand 15
saw 23
seal 15
seaweed 15
seed drill 9
sheep 13
sheep-dip 7
sheepdog 9
shell 15
shepherd 9
shoots 11

shovel 9
silo 7
snow 23
squirrel 21
stable 7
starfish 15
straw 17
stream 5
swallow 13
swimming 17

T

tadpoles 11
toadstool 21
tractor 9

V

valley 5
village 5

W

wall 7
waterfall 5
wheat 17
wheelbarrow 9
wood 5
wood pigeon 21
woollen hat 23

Other books you may enjoy:

Age 3+
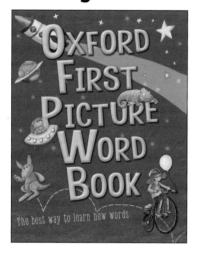

Age 4+
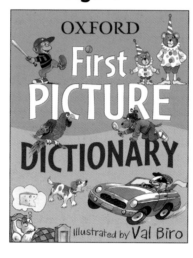

Age 4+
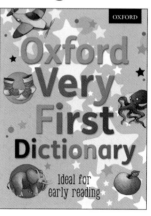

Age 5+

Age 5+
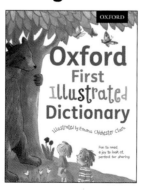

Age 5+
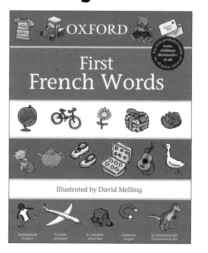

Age 5+
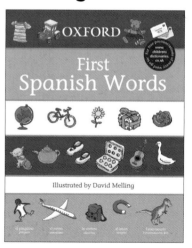

BENVENUTO AL MONDO, BEBÈ !

Welcome to the World Baby

Na'ima bint Robert

Illustrated by Derek Brazell

Italian translation by Patrizia Zambrin

Un lunedì mattina, Tariq arrivò a scuola con un enorme sorriso in volto.

"Indovinate cosa, tutti?" esclamò. "Sabato mi sono svegliato e il mio nuovo fratellino era nel letto di mia mamma!"

On Monday morning, Tariq came to school with a huge smile on his face. "Guess what, everyone?" he cried. "I woke up on Saturday and my new baby brother was in my mum's bed!"

I bambini erano eccitati. Avevano visto la mamma di Tariq diventare sempre più grossa. Avevano aspettato il gran giorno.

The children were excited. They had seen Tariq's mum getting bigger and bigger and bigger. They had been waiting for the big day.

"Cosa c'è in quella borsa, Tariq?" chiese la maestra, la signorina Smith. "La mamma mi ha dato questi datteri da spartire con tutti. Noi diamo ad un nuovo bebè un morbido pezzo di dattero, la primissima cosa che assaggia."

"What's in the bag, Tariq?" asked his teacher, Miss Smith.
"My mum gave me these dates to share with everyone. We give a new baby a soft piece of date, the first thing they will ever taste."

I bambini mangiarono tutti un dattero.
Mmm, era dolce e liscio.

The children all had a date.
Hmmm, it tasted sweet and smooth.

I bambini avevano imparato i cinque sensi a scuola e tutti conoscevano il gusto, il tatto, la vista, l'udito e l'odorato.

The children had been learning about the five senses in school and they all knew about tasting, touching, seeing, hearing and smelling.

"Quanti di voi hanno avuto un nuovo fratellino o una nuova sorellina recentemente?" chiese la signorina Smith.
Parecchie mani si alzarono.

"How many of you have had a new baby brother or sister recently?" asked Miss Smith.
Quite a few hands shot up.

"Perchè non chiedete ai vostri genitori come si accolgono i nuovi bebè nella vostra famiglia? Potreste portare qualcosa venerdì e parlarcene," disse la signorina Smith.

"Can you ask your parents how you welcome new babies in your family? Maybe you can all bring something in on Friday and tell us about it," said Miss Smith.

"Possiamo portare qualsiasi cosa?" chiese Ben.
"Sì, Ben. Qualsiasi cosa volete, basta che abbia
a che fare con i cinque sensi!"

"Can we bring anything?" asked Ben.
"Yes, Ben. Anything you like, as long as it's to do
with the five senses!"

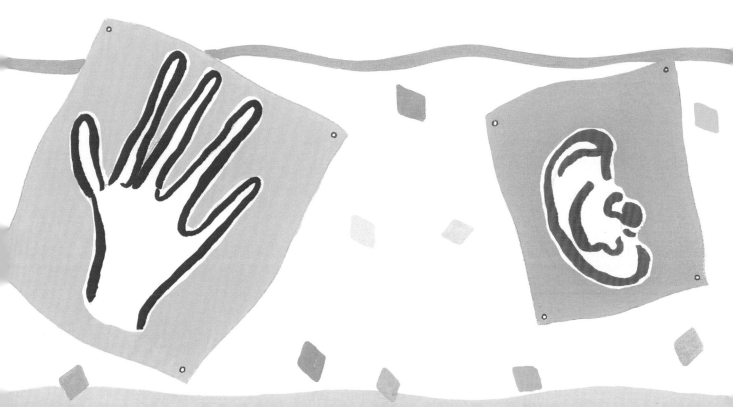

Venerdì, tutti i bambini vennero
a scuola con qualcosa davvero speciale.
La signorina Smith li fece sedere in circolo.
"Ora bambini," incominciò, "molti di noi sanno
quanto sia meraviglioso avere un nuovo bebè in
famiglia. Per tutti è tempo di gran gioia e festa.
Scopriamo com'è essere un nuovo bebè nelle
reciproche case."

On Friday, all the children came to school with something extra special.
Miss Smith sat them down in a circle.
"Now children," she began, "many of us know how wonderful it is to have
a new baby in the family. For everyone it's a time of great joy and
celebration. Let's find out what it's like to be a new baby in
each other's homes."

"Allora, An-Mei, cosa succede quando nasce un nuovo bebè in casa tua?" chiese.

Con molta cura An-Mei tirò fuori un uovo, un piccolo uovo, dipinto di rosso.

"So, An-Mei, what happens when a new baby is born in your house?" she asked.

Very carefully An-Mei brought out an egg, a little egg, painted red.

"Questo è uno delle uova che la mamma e il papà diedero in dono alla famiglia e agli amici. È dipinto di rosso, il colore della buona fortuna. L'uovo sta per la nascita, la vita e la crescita. Toccalo con le mani," disse, passandolo a Brian.

"This is one of the eggs that my mum and dad gave as gifts to our family and friends. It is painted red, the colour of good luck. The egg stands for birth, life and growth. Touch it with your hands," she said, passing it to Brian.

"È liscio, come la faccia della mamma,"
disse Brian, accarezzando l'ovetto fresco.
Tutti gli altri bambini sorrisero.
"Ora, a chi tocca?" chiese la
signorina Smith.

"It's so smooth, just like my mum's face," said Brian,
stroking the cool little egg.
The other children all smiled.
"Now, who's next?" asked Miss Smith.

Lentamente, Saida aprì una piccola busta bianca e tirò fuori una ciocca di capelli, una ciocca di capelli scuri e ricci, legati con un nastro bianco.

Slowly, Saida opened a small white envelope and took out a lock of hair, a lock of curly dark hair, tied with a white ribbon.

"Questi sono dei capelli di mio fratellino conservati dopo che Amma e Abba gli rasarono la testa, quando aveva solo sette giorni di vita."

"Perchè?" chiese Ben.

"Per portarli dall'orefice a pesarli. Poi diedero il loro peso in argento ai poveri," disse Saida.

"This is some of my baby brother's first hair that was kept after Amma and Abba shaved my brother's head, when he was only seven days old."

"Why?" asked Ben.

"So that they could take it to the jewellers and weigh it. Then they gave its weight in silver to help the poor," said Saida.

Lo passò a Caroline. "Toccali con le dita," disse. "I primi capelli di mio fratellino…"
"Sono così leggeri e soffici," disse Caroline, accarezzando il piccolo ricciolo.

She passed it to Caroline. "Feel it with your fingers," she said.
"My baby brother's first hair…"
"It's so light and soft," Caroline said, stroking the little curl.

Poi fu il turno di Dimitri.
Aprì una scatoletta. C'erano monete
dentro, monete d'oro e d'argento,
che brillavano nella scatola scura.

Next it was Dimitri's turn. He opened a small box.
In it were coins, gold and silver coins,
shining in the dark box.

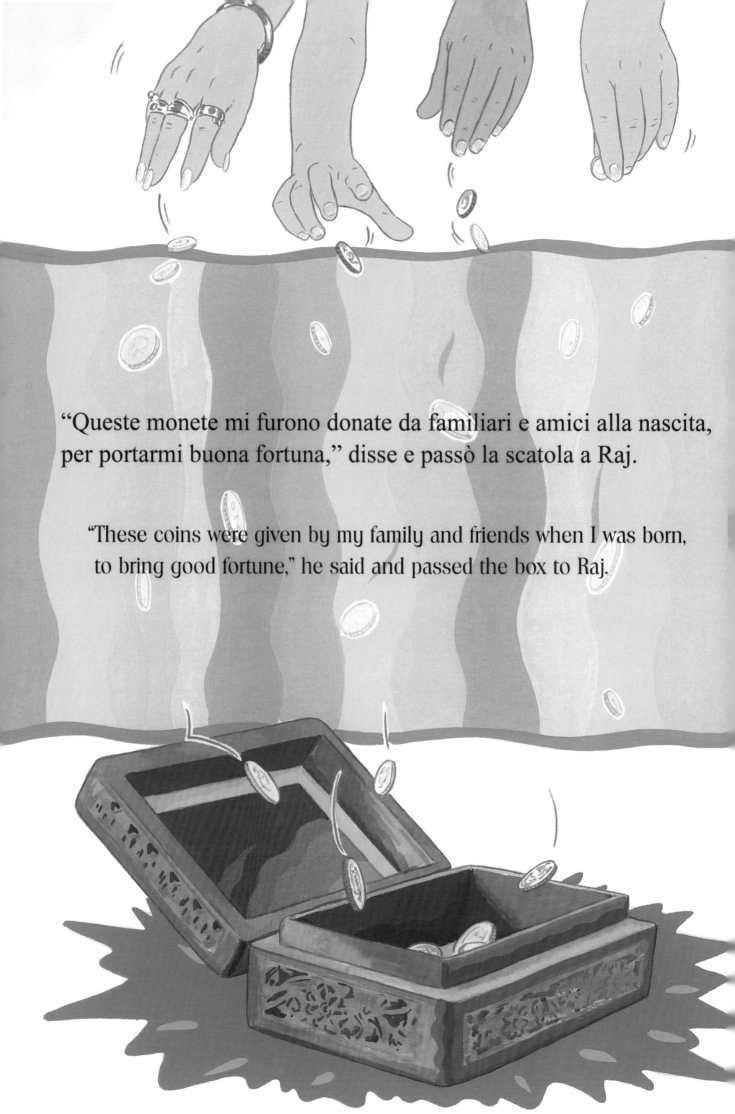

"Queste monete mi furono donate da familiari e amici alla nascita, per portarmi buona fortuna," disse e passò la scatola a Raj.

"These coins were given by my family and friends when I was born, to bring good fortune," he said and passed the box to Raj.

"Scuoti la scatola e ascolta il suono che fanno le monete."
"Tintinnano!" urlò Raj, avvicinando l'orecchio alla scatola.

"Shake the box and listen to the sound the coins make."
"It jingle-jangles!" cried Raj, putting his ear close to the box.

Nadia si mise a parlare, timidamente.
"Signorina," disse, "io ho qualcosa."
Prese una borsa e tirò fuori un maglione, un grande e caldo
maglione che sembrava avere ricevuto molto amore.

Nadia spoke up, shyly.
"Miss," she said, "I've got something."
She picked up a bag and pulled out
a jumper, a big warm jumper that looked
as though it had seen a lot of love.

"Questo è il maglione di mio papà," disse. "Quando sono nata,
ci fui avvolta dentro, e ricevetti tre nomi speciali."

"This is my dad's jumper," she said. "When I was born, I was
wrapped in it, and given three special names."

Lo passò a Sara.
"Chiudi gli occhi e annusalo," sussurrò. "Sa di forte e sicuro come mio papà."

She passed it to Sara.
"Close your eyes and smell it," she whispered. "It smells strong and safe like my dad."

Sara chiuse gli occhi e inspirò profondamente. "Mmm," sospirò, "che buon profumo per un neonato!"

Sara closed her eyes and breathed in deeply. "Hmmm," she sighed, "what a lovely smell for a newborn baby!"

Infine fu la volta di Elima.

Dalla sua borsa, tirò fuori una foglia, una piccola foglia di aloe.

"Quando sono nato, mi è stato dato un po' di questo," disse.

"Assaggialo."

Lo spremette e un po' di succo cadde sulle dita di Mona.

Finally it was Elima's turn.

From his bag, he brought out a leaf, a small aloe leaf.

"When I was born, I was given some of this," he said. "Taste it."

He squeezed it and some juice fell onto Mona's fingers.

Lo assaggiò con entusiasmo. "Puah! È così amaro," strillò, asciugandosi la bocca.

Eagerly she tasted it. "Urghh! It's *so* bitter," she cried, wiping her mouth.

"Questo è per insegnare al bebè che la vita può essere amara ma…" disse, tirando fuori un vasetto di miele, "può essere anche dolce!"

"That is to teach the baby that life can be bitter, but…" he said, bringing out a little pot of honey, "it can also be sweet!"

Mona si liberò in fretta del gusto di aloe con un cucchiaino di delizioso miele.

Mona was quick to get rid of the aloe taste with a spoonful of delicious honey.

"Signorina!" urlò Kwesi, "abbiamo usato tutti i nostri sensi, vero?"
"Proprio così, Kwesi," disse la signorina Smith, con un enorme sorriso in volto.

"Miss!" cried Kwesi, "we've used all of our senses, haven't we?"
"That's right, Kwesi," said Miss Smith, with a huge smile on her face.

"Bravi, tutti quanti! Come speciale ricompensa, faremo una
festa dei Cinque Sensi alla fine del trimestre."
"Evviva!" esclamarono tutti.
"E," disse la signorina Smith, "avremo un ospite a sorpresa."
Tutti si chiesero chi potesse essere.

"Well done, all of you! As a special treat, we'll have a Five Senses party
at the end of term."
"Hooray!" they all cheered.
"And," said Miss Smith, "we'll have a surprise visitor."
They all wondered who that could be.

L'ultimo giorno del trimestre, mentre i bambini si godevano la loro speciale festa dei Cinque Sensi, qualcuno bussò alla porta. "Chi può essere?" chiese la signorina Smith con un gran sorriso.

On the last day of term, while the children were enjoying their special Five Senses party, there was a knock at the door.
"Who can that be?" asked Miss Smith with a big smile.

Lentamente la porta si aprì.

Era la mamma di Tariq con…il nuovo bebè!

I bambini applaudirono.

"Benvenuto al mondo, bebè, benvenuto al mondo!" cantarono tutti.

Slowly the door opened.
It was Tariq's mum with...the new baby!
The children cheered.
"Welcome to the world, baby, welcome to
the world!" they all sang.

La mamma di Tariq e il suo nuovo fratellino entrarono e si unirono alla festa.
E sapete, fu il piu bel benvenuto che un bebe abbia mai ricevuto!

Tariq's mum and his new baby brother came and joined the party.
And do you know, it was the nicest welcome any baby had ever had!